Coyote's soundbite

John Agard

Piet Grobler

 Lantana

The breaking news spread like bushfire
among all the animals of the rainforest.
Earth-goddesses were planning a conference!

Excitement buzzed the air, as you can guess.
The animals perked up ears, tails, feathers,
spikes, horns, bristles, whatever!

There they stood on forelegs, on hindlegs,
on tip-toe flippers, you name it!
The animals couldn't wait, couldn't wait.

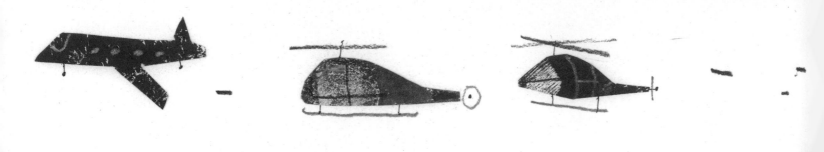

The coming conference of earth-goddesses
from far-flung corners of the planet
was going to be the first of its kind.

And of course, the big burning issue
the conference would discuss and ponder
was whether humans are blind

or have simply lost their mind?
The earth-goddesses should have some clue,
for they were all known to be very wise.

On earth they'd keep their watchful eyes.
Down to a butterfly's silent flutter,
down to the coming alive of a flower

in the sun-blessed light of spring,
down to a golden ear of corn ripening,
a tiny seed waking in a cradle of darkness,

a snail on a leaf softly spiralling,
a mole in deep-down burrow unwinding:
the earth-goddesses never miss a thing.

But even bushy-tailed, smooth-talking Coyote,
who had travelled the world over
and always saw himself as a globe-trotter,

was still to meet an earth-goddess face to face.
So you can imagine Coyote's disappointment
when he heard that only the female creatures

would be allowed at the historic event.
Not even the male earth-gods (no disrespect)
were welcome on this particular occasion.

Since nothing ventured, nothing gained,
Coyote decided on the spur of the moment
that he'd put on his wife's blue dress.

A bit on the tight side, but would surely do.
Besides, the dress went well with the toeless
high-heeled shoes and turquoise handbag.

Out stepped Coyote with a zig and a zag.
Mistaking Coyote for a high-class lady,
two Ravens ushered him to the front row.

Then the chair-goddess announced herself.
Darana, she-whose-singing-gave-birth-to-rain,
had travelled from the land of the didgeridoo.

To much applause, but without much ado,
Darana recalled how from her belly-button
had sprouted the very first witchetty grub

for the first-ever humans to feed on.
Darana and humans then spoke one tongue.
So it was in the dream-time beginning,

before the riches of Darana's dark veins
had become divided into losses and gains.
With that, Darana introduced Oduduwa.

Emerging from her calabash of ebony,
Oduduwa said she'd keep it short and sweet.
All she wished was to jolt human memory.

"Let them go ask the tree of sixteen branches,
from whose flesh grew the first kola nut
when first-humans toddled on their butt."

Imagining first-humans toddling on their butt
did make Coyote give a little grin.
A laugh out-loud would be embarrassing!

Next came the earth-goddess Kujum Chantu,
who spoke of wonders of which legends told:
legends passed on to the young from the old.

How her eyes grew into the sun and moon.
How her bones became hills. How her breast
became what's known today as Mount Everest.

But most marvellous of all her telling
was how Kujum Chantu's own belly fat
became home-ground for first-humans to squat.

Although the conference day had been sunny,
the next speaker wore fur boots and fur coat
with leather trimmings down to her knees.

She was, of course, from the land of permafrost
where folk were used to the igloo for a home.
She introduced herself as earth-goddess Ninam.

"Forgive me, my friends, if I, Ninam, shed a tear.
I grieve for the polar bear, my iceberg-rider,
for the walrus, my tooth-walking-sea-horse.

When human doing destroys their feeding grounds,
when their home-sweet-home ice is no more,
I ask, can my beloved creatures survive for long?"

Next to speak was Brigid, keeper of the wells,
whose waters spring from the womb of earth.
A daughter of Moon Mother, Brigid tends

the fire for the storyteller's word-weaving.
But with their forest hide-outs disappearing,
the fairy people are up and leaving.

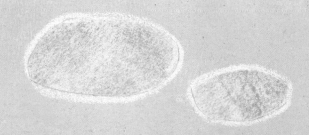

Brigid went on to welcome, live and direct
from the Andes where roam the beautiful llama,
none other than earth-goddess Panchamama.

Panchamama was in no mood for endless talk.
Panchamama was all for walking the walk.
She was one earth-mama who'd tell it as it was.

"These humans forget how mother earth grieves
when her rainforests weep in their own ash
and her oceans are garlanded in trash."

Panchamama's words made the animals reply
with a chorus of howls, shrieks, screeches,
resounding roars that pierced the ears of sky.

That was when the chair-goddess Darana
invited the gathering to ask any questions.
A heavy silence fell. Neither question nor answer.

The silence felt like forever and ever.
Then Coyote, of course, thought it clever
to come up with some sort of a suggestion.

"Excuse me, ladies! Forgive my interjection,
but from my study of the human breed,
I'll say a soundbite is what you ladies need!"

In case soundbite should cause any bother,
Coyote explained that soundbite was the tool
the humans use to get a message over.

"How about this, ladies, for a suggestion?

Earth-lovers of the world unite!
Mother Nature is always right!"

All agreed the soundbite had a certain ring.
The front-seat lady with the turquoise handbag
definitely knew what she was talking.

When he got back home, Coyote was well surprised.
He couldn't believe what greeted his eyes.
There stood Coyote's wife (and this is the truth)

all dressed up in Coyote's three-piece tweed suit,
complete with two-toned shoes and polka dot tie.
She seemed ever so pleased with her disguise.

Then Mrs Coyote had to explain to her hubbie
that she'd just got back from a conference
of male earth-gods (goddess wives weren't allowed).

"But I just thought I'd put in an appearance,"
Mrs Coyote said, winking towards Mr Coyote.
"My blue dress suits you by the way," she added.

"Is there something you're not telling me?"
Coyote asked (for he was busy imagining
his wife in male dress at a males-only gathering).

"Oh, I suggested to the earth-gods a soundbite:

Earth-lovers of the world unite!
Mother Nature is always right!"

All Mr and Mrs Coyote did at that moment
was look at each other with approving eyes
and say, "Yes dear, great minds do think alike."

To The Great Earth-Spirit - JA

In memory of my parents Cor and Hanna Grobler who
taught me to love the earth - PG

First published in the United Kingdom in 2021 by Lantana Publishing Ltd., Oxford.
www.lantanapublishing.com | info@lantanapublishing.com

American edition published in 2021 by Lantana Publishing Ltd., UK.

Text © John Agard, 2021
Illustration © Piet Grobler, 2021

Distributed in the United States and Canada by Lerner Publishing Group, Inc.
241 First Avenue North, Minneapolis, MN 55401 U.S.A.
For reading levels and more information, look for this title at www.lernerbooks.com
Cataloging-in-Publication Data Available.

Printed and bound in China.
Original mixed media collage using colored pencils, ink and gouache.

Hardcover ISBN: 978-1-911373-73-5
PDF ISBN: 978-1-911373-77-3
Trade ePub3 ISBN: 978-1-913747-61-9
S&L ePub3 ISBN: 978-1-913747-49-7